Max Velthuijs

 KU-754-777

青蛙和陌生人
Frog and the Stranger

Chinese translation by David Tsai

MILET

STAFFORDSHIRE LIBRARIES ARTS AND ARCHIVES	
38014040227933	
PET	12-Jan-06
CF	£7.99
BURT	

一天，來了一個陌生人，在樹林邊上扎了個帳篷。是小豬最先發現他的。

One day, a stranger arrived and made a camp at the edge of the woods. It was Pig who discovered him first.

"你看到他了嗎？" 小豬遇到鴨子和青蛙時激動地問道。
"還沒有。他長的什麼樣？" 鴨子又問道。
"如果你是在問我，那我說他看上去就像一隻齷齪、骯髒的老鼠，" 小豬回答說。
"他到這兒來干什麼？"
"你對老鼠們得當心點，" 鴨子說。 "他們到處偷東西。"

"Have you seen him?" asked Pig excitedly when he met Duck and Frog.
"No. What's he like?" asked Duck.
"If you ask me, he looks like a filthy dirty rat," said Pig. "What does he want here?"
"You have to be careful of rats," said Duck. "They're a thieving lot."

"你怎麼知道的？"青蛙詢問道。 "每個人都知道，"鴨子憤憤地說道。
但是，青蛙卻不是那麼肯定。他要親自看一看。那天晚上，當夜幕降臨之後，他看
到遠處有紅光在閃爍。青蛙躡手躡腳地向它逐漸靠近。

"How do you know?" asked Frog. "Everyone knows," said Duck indignantly.
But Frog wasn't so sure. He wanted to see for himself. That night, when darkness fell he
saw a red glow in the distance. Frog crept nearer.

在樹林邊上他看到一個用幾根棍棒支撐著一塊地毯所搭成的不整齊的帳篷，像個臨時代用品。

At the edge of the wood he saw a couple of sticks with a rag draped over them, like a makeshift, untidy tent.

那個陌生人正在火上的鍋中做飯。從那兒飄來了一股香味,青蛙覺得一切看上去都很舒適。

The stranger was cooking in a pot over a fire. There was a wonderful smell and Frog thought it all looked very cosy.

"我看到他了，" 第二天，青蛙把這事兒告訴給大家。
"然後呢？" 小豬追問道。"他看上去像是個好人，" 青蛙說道。

"I've seen him," Frog told the others, next day.
"And?" asked Pig. "He looks like a nice fellow," said Frog.

"當心點，" 小豬說。"別忘了他是隻骯髒的老鼠。"
"我敢說，他甚至連一天的工夫都不用就會把我們所有的食物全吃光的，"
鴨子說道。"老鼠們又貪又懶。"

"Be careful," said Pig. "Remember he's a dirty rat."
"I bet he'll eat all our food without ever doing a day's work," said Duck.
"Rats are cheeky and lazy."

但那說的不對。老鼠總是忙忙碌碌的。他採來了木頭然後嫻熟地做成了餐桌和長條凳。他其實也不骯髒。他經常在河裡洗澡，雖然他看上去有點不整潔。

But that wasn't true. Rat was always busy. He collected wood and skilfully made a table and bench. He wasn't really dirty either. He often bathed in the river although he looked a little scruffy.

一天，青蛙決定去訪問老鼠。老鼠正坐在他新制做的長條凳上在陽光中休息。"你好，"青蛙問候說。"我是青蛙。""我知道，"老鼠回答說。"我可以看的出來。我還不蠢。我即會讀又會寫，我還能講三種語言－英語、法語和德語。"青蛙得到的印象太深刻了。甚至連野兔都不會這麼多。

One day, Frog decided to visit Rat. Rat was sitting resting on his new bench in the sun. "Hello," said Frog. "I'm Frog." "I know," said Rat. "I can see that. I'm not stupid. I can read and write and I speak three languages – English, French and German." Frog was very impressed. Even Hare couldn't do that.

小豬剛好在那時到達了。
"你是從哪個地方來的？" 他生氣地問老鼠說。
"從每個地方和無地方，" 老鼠平靜地回答說。
"好吧，那你為什麼不回去呢？" 小豬大聲地說道。 "這兒沒有你可做的事。"
老鼠依然保持平靜。

Just then, Pig arrived.
"Where are you from?" he asked Rat angrily.
"From everywhere and nowhere," replied Rat calmly.
"Well, why don't you go back?" cried Pig. "You've no business here."
Rat remained calm.

"我已經走遍了天下，" 老鼠堅定地說。"這裡十分安寧，河上有美麗的景色。我喜歡這裡。"

"I have travelled all over the world," said Rat unmoved. "It's peaceful here and there's a wonderful view over to the river. I like it here."

"我敢肯定你偷了木頭，" 小豬說道。"是我找到的，" 老鼠用氣憤的聲音回答說。"它屬於每一個人。""骯髒的老鼠，" 小豬低聲說道。
"對，對，" 老鼠痛苦地說道。"每一件事總是我的錯。對任何事情老鼠總是受責怪的。"

"I bet you stole the wood," said Pig. "I found it," said Rat in a dignified voice. "It belongs to everyone." "Dirty rat," muttered Pig.
"Yes, yes," said Rat bitterly. "Everything is always my fault. Rat is always blamed for everything."

青蛙、小豬和鴨子來訪問野兔。 "那隻齷齪的老鼠必須離開，" 小豬說。 "他沒權力待在這裡。他偷了我們的木頭，還蠻不講理，" 鴨子嚷道。 "安靜點，安靜點，" 野兔說。 "他可能跟我們有些不同，但是他沒做什麼錯事，而且木頭是屬於大家的。"

Frog, Pig and Duck went to visit Hare. "That filthy rat must leave," said Pig. "He's no right to be here. He steals our wood and is rude as well," cried Duck. "Quiet, quiet," said Hare. "He may be different from us, but he's not doing anything wrong and the wood belongs to everyone."

從那天開始，青蛙按時去訪問老鼠。他們在長條凳上並肩而坐，欣賞著景色。老鼠還把他週遊世界的冒險故事拿來講，因為他畢竟遊覽四方有好多激動人心的經歷

From that day on, Frog went to visit Rat regularly. They sat side by side on the bench, enjoying the view and Rat told Frog stories of his adventures round the world, for he had travelled widely and had had many exciting experiences.

小豬不贊成青蛙。 "你不應該跟那隻齷齪的老鼠到處亂轉," 他說。
"為什麼不應該?" 青蛙責問道。 "因為他跟我們不一樣," 鴨子說道。
"不一樣," 青蛙說道, "可是我們都不一樣啊。"
"不," 鴨子說。 "我們是屬於一起的。可老鼠不生在這裡。"

Pig disapproved of Frog. "You shouldn't go round with that filthy rat," he said.
"Why not?" asked Frog. "Because he's different from us," said Duck.
"Different," said Frog, "but we're all different."
"No," said Duck. "We belong together. Rat isn't from round here."

然後有一天，小豬做飯時沒有留心。火苗在煎鍋裡跳躍。很快火焰向四處蔓延，到處都是火。整座房子成了一片火海。

Then one day, Pig was careless while he was cooking. Flames leapt from the frying pan. Soon the fire spread and the flames were everywhere. The house was ablaze.

他跑出去後嚇壞了。 "起火了！起火了！" 他聲嘶力竭地喊叫著。但是老鼠早就
到了。他提著一桶桶的水在河水與房子之間奔波著，與烈火進行搏鬥，直到大火
被撲滅。

He ran outside terrified. "Fire! Fire!" he screamed. But Rat was already there. He hurried
between the river and the house with buckets of water and fought the flames until the
fire was out.

小豬房子的屋頂被全部燒壞了。所有的動物站在那兒驚呆了。小豬現在變成了無家可歸。不過他用不著擔心。第二天，老鼠帶著錘子和釘子來了。三下五去二，不到一會兒房子便給修好了！

The roof of Pig's house was totally destroyed. All the animals stood round in shock. Now Pig was homeless. But he needn't have worried. The next day, Rat came round with a hammer and nails. As quick as a flash, the house was repaired!

還有一次，野兔去河邊取水。
他突然滑倒落入深水之中。野兔不會游泳。
"救命啊！救命啊！" 他大聲呼喊著。
是老鼠先聽到了呼喊聲，並立刻潛入水中。很快，他便營救了野兔，並且把他帶到
安全、乾燥的河岸上。

Another time, Hare went to the river to fetch some water.
Suddenly he slipped and fell into deep water. Hare couldn't swim.
"Help! Help!" he shouted loudly.
It was Rat who heard the shouts at once and dived straight into the water. Quickly he
rescued Hare and brought him to the safe, dry bank.

每個人現在都同意老鼠可以留下來。他一貫性格開朗、心情快活，而且當有人需要幫助時，他總是在那兒。

Everyone now agreed that Rat could stay. He was constantly happy and cheerful and was always there if someone needed help.

他經常在構思做一些有趣的事情，像安排在河邊吃野餐、或組織一次森林郊遊等。

He often thought of fun things to do like having a picnic by the river or a trip into the forest.

在晚間，他給他們講些關於中國龍的激動人心的故事—他在世界遇到的另一件令人激動的事情。這是段美好的時光，老鼠總是有講不完的新故事。

And during the evenings, he told them all exciting stories about dragons in China and other exciting things he had encountered in the world. It was a very happy time and Rat always had new tales to tell.

但在風和日麗一天，當青蛙到他的朋友老鼠家訪問時，他不能相信他的眼睛。
帳篷已經拆除了，老鼠帶著他的背包正站那兒。

But one fine day when Frog visited his friend Rat he couldn't believe his eyes.
The tent had been taken down and Rat was standing there with his rucksack.

"你要走嗎？" 青蛙大惑不解地問道。
"到了該走動的時候了，" 老鼠解釋說。 "我或許會去美洲。我還從未去過那兒。"
青蛙感到不知所措。

"Are you leaving?" asked Frog in amazement.
"It's time to move on," said Rat. "I might go to America. I've never been there."
Frog was devastated.

青蛙、鴨子、野兔和小豬眼裡含著眼淚，與他們的朋友老鼠揮手說了再見。
"我大概有一天還會回來的，"老鼠快活地說道。"到那時我會在河上建一座橋的。"

With tears in their eyes, Frog, Duck, Hare and Pig said goodbye to their friend Rat. "Perhaps I'll come back one day," said Rat cheerfully. "Then I'll build a bridge over the river."

然後他便離開了－那隻齷齪、骯髒，但卻好心、大方、樂於助人、聰明的老鼠。
他們目送著他的身影，直到他消失在山丘的背後。"我們會想念他的，"
野兔感觸地說道。

Then he left – that filthy dirty, but nice, cheeky, helpful, clever Rat. They stared after him until he disappeared behind the hill. "We'll miss him," said Hare with a sigh.

是的，老鼠在身後留下一塊空地。但是長條凳依然還在，四個朋友經常一起坐在上
面反覆談論著他們記憶中的好朋友老鼠。

Yes, Rat left an empty space behind. But the bench was still there and the four friends often sat together on it and talked over their memories of their good friend Rat.